SHADOW DANCE

by Tololwa M. Mollel

Illustrated by Donna Perrone

Clarion Books

NEW YORK

Clarion Books
a Houghton Mifflin Company imprint
215 Park Avenue South, New York, NY 10003
Text copyright © 1998 by Tololwa M. Mollel
Illustrations copyright © 1998 by Donna Perrone

Illustrations executed in oil crayons and color pencils on paper.
Type is 15/20 pt. Meridian Medium.

Printed in Singapore.

Library of Congress Cataloging-in-Publication Data

Mollel, Tololwa M. (Tololwa Marti)
Shadow dance / by Tololwa M. Mollel ; illustrated by Donna Perrone.
p.   cm.
Summary: When the crocodile she has rescued tricks her, little Salome
must use some cunning of her own to escape becoming his meal.
ISBN 0-395-82909-7
[1. Folklore—Africa.] I. Perrone, Donna, ill. II. Title.
PZ8.1.M73Sh   1998
398.2'96'02—dc20
[E]   96-47332
CIP
AC

TWP 10 9 8 7 6 5 4 3 2 1

To Joanne Kellock.
—T.M.M.

To Eleanor Tauber, my angel,
Thank you for being there for me. You have always held
your arms open for me. I admire your strength, your
courage, and your keen awareness of what is real.

Special thanks to Dinah Stevenson, Eleanor Voorhees,
and Anne Diebel at Clarion for their great direction
in creating this book!
—D.P.

After a long rainy season, the sun smiled down upon the earth. Flooded fields dried and bloomed under a clear sky.

In a field near a river, little Salome rejoiced. She skipped and hopped and danced with her shadow, and she sang a joyful song.

Kivuli pere pepere
Kivuli wee pere pepere
Oye oyee pere peperee
Kivuli wee pere pepere

Mwenzangu pere pepere
Mwenzangu wee pere pepere
Oye oyee pere peperee
Mwenzangu wee pere pepere,

Salome sang.

All at once, she stopped.

She heard the cry of someone in trouble. "Help, help!" Salome stared through the bushes.

Trapped in a gully behind the bushes was an enormous crocodile, who stared back sadly at Salome. "My dear girl," he said, "I'll thank you very much if you'll be kind enough to help me out of this gully. Floodwaters washed me from the river and stranded me here."

He sounded so weak and harmless, Salome felt sorry for him. It took only moments and a few vine ropes for the clever girl to pull Crocodile out of the gully.

Crocodile groaned. "My dear girl," he said, "I'll thank you even more if you'll kindly walk me to my home in the river. I've grown stiff and sore, trapped for so long."

He sounded so miserable, Salome couldn't say no. Gently and patiently she walked him to the river.

At the riverbank, Crocodile sighed. "My dear girl," he said, "I'll thank you even more if you'll be so kind as to steady me down into the cooling waters. The sun has so scorched me, I am dying with weariness."

And indeed he looked so sun-baked and withered, Salome agreed to help. Carefully she steadied him down into the water, and there in one swift movement Crocodile grabbed her.

Salome struggled
and wriggled and tore in
vain at Crocodile's iron grip. "No,
please spare me!" she cried.

Crocodile laughed. "Well, my dear girl,
tell me one good reason why a big hungry
crocodile like me should spare a little girl like you."

"Ungrateful beast!" Salome screamed. "Who freed you from the gully? Who walked you to the river? Who steadied you down to the water? I did, I did, I did! That's more than enough reason!"

"Not good enough," Crocodile replied. Then he chuckled slyly. "I'll be fair, though. If I can find a better reason to spare you, I'll let you go."

A little upstream, they came to a gnarled old tree by the river. Crocodile asked the tree, "Can you give me one good reason, O ancient one, why a big hungry crocodile should spare a little girl?"

"Spare her?" exclaimed the tree. "Little girls deserve no pity! Once, years ago, some little girls came to me. Day after day I let them play hide-and-seek among my

branches. When they got hungry, I fed them fruit. I sheltered them from the sting of the sun and the lash of the rain.

"From the magic of their joy, I flourished. I grew heavy with fruit and tall to the clouds. My branches spread far and wide and attracted birds of every kind.

"Then suddenly one day . . .

". . . the little girls left me for another tree. Abandoned me! With their magic gone, my fine leaves dwindled, my tall trunk hunched, and my proud branches shriveled.

The birds left with their cheerful songs and lovely nests.
I became lonely and ugly." The tree shed three bitter leafy
tears. "No, Crocodile, don't spare the little girl."

"The wicked tree blames me for something I didn't do," said Salome. "I wasn't one of those girls. It's not fair. Ask someone else."

Farther upstream, they met a withered old cow drinking water. Crocodile asked her the same question.

"Little girls deserve no mercy, for they grow up to be mean," said the cow. "Once, when I was young, I was treated like a queen, only because I had milk to give for Master's little daughter. I was given tasty corn mush and salt bars, clean water, and a soft straw bed. Children stroked my neck and sang gentle songs for me.

"Feeding on my milk, Master's little daughter grew into a big girl. The big girl grew into a woman, and mistress of the farm, while I grew old and dry of milk.

"All is changed for me now. No more corn mush and

salt bars. No more clean water and soft straw. No more stroking or gentle songs. With only a short break for a munch of prickly grass and a drink of muddy water, Mistress puts me to plow her fields all day. As if I were an ox! No, Crocodile, don't spare the little girl."

"It's not my fault the silly cow is unhappy!" Salome told Crocodile. "You must ask someone else."

Just then, a cheery voice spoke.

"I can give you *a dozen* good reasons why you should spare the little girl."

A pigeon hopped into sight on a nearby bush.

Crocodile gave the pigeon a haughty glance. "Don't bother," he replied smugly. "Nothing on earth would make me spare her."

"But you promised!" Salome exclaimed.

"Never trust a hungry crocodile." Crocodile laughed a rumbling laugh. "It was all a game, my dear girl." He turned to the pigeon. "All a game."

"Suit yourself," replied the pigeon. "But before you have your lunch, Crocodile, tell me something. Your home is in the river. The little girl lives on land. I'm curious—how in the world did you meet?"

Crocodile loved telling stories. "It all happened," he began, "after floodwaters washed me from the river and stranded me in a gully. There I lay trapped when—"

"You're lying," Salome said. "You were not trapped."

"I'm not lying," Crocodile shot back. "I was trapped in the gully until you came along."

"You just pretended to be trapped so you could catch me. Liar!"

"Liar yourself. I was not pretending, and you know it!"

Salome turned to the pigeon. "I'll show you just what happened, and you'll see for yourself who is lying."

"No, *I'll* show you what *really* happened," Crocodile told the pigeon, "and you'll see for yourself who is lying!"

The pigeon, exchanging glances with Salome, was quick to agree.

They returned to the gully. Confidently, Crocodile crawled back inside. After trying to climb out, he shouted up in triumph, "See, I *am* trapped. I told the truth!"

"So you did, so you did, Crocodile," replied the pigeon.

Singing, Salome danced away,
the pigeon on her shoulder.
Then, all at once, she stopped
to listen to the cry of someone
in *deep* trouble. "Help, help!"

Salome did not so much as look back. Heading home, she skipped and hopped and danced with her shadow, and she sang a joyful song.

Kivuli pere pepere
Kivuli wee pere pepere
Oye oyee pere peperee
Kivuli wee pere pepere

Mwenzangu pere pepere
Mwenzangu wee pere pepere
Oye oyee pere peperee
Mwenzangu wee pere pepere,

Salome sang.

AUTHOR'S NOTE

Shadow Dance is based on a cross-cultural theme that I have found in African, European, and Asian tales—the ungrateful captive who victimizes his rescuer. A third party saves the victim by tricking the ingrate back into captivity. I have given the theme a twist in *Shadow Dance*: Spunky Salome (sah LO meh) saves herself through her own resourcefulness, turning from victim into trickster with the pigeon's help. I have placed the story in modern Tanzania, instead of a timeless, "neutral" folktale setting, and given it a contemporary protagonist.

The song that begins and ends the story is in Kiswahili, Tanzania's national language. I adapted it from a song that traditionally goes along with energetic, rhythmic team activities like marching, jogging, or rowing.

Kivuli wee (kee VOO lee weh): Hey (you), shadow!

Mwenzangu wee (mwenn ZAHNG goo weh): Hey (you), my companion!

Oyee oyee (oh yeh oh yeh): Hooray, hooray!

Pere pepere (peh reh peh PEH reh): A nonsense refrain like "tra la la."

Transcribed by Paul Alan Levi

The words *kivuli* and *mwenzangu* can be replaced with other Kiswahili words to add more verses to the song at the end of the story: *rafiki* (rah FEE kee), friend; *shogangu* (shoh GAHNG goo), my buddy (said by a girl about another girl); *dadangu* (duh DUNG goo), my sister. Singing along and dancing with others, or with your shadow, you can celebrate with Salome for a grand finale.